Robert Sheckley's first science fiction and fantasy stories were published in 1951 while he was still at the University of New York. In 1952, after working for six months as an X-ray technician in an aircraft plant, he became a full-time writer. His books include *Immortality Inc*, *Journey Beyond Tomorrow*, *Mindswap*, and *The People Trap*.

Born in 1928, Robert Sheckley was brought up in New Jersey. He lives with his wife in New York and has a great lust for travelling – when not on a trip, he is always planning the next one.

THE SAME TO YOU DOUBLED

AND OTHER STORIES

(Previously published as
Can You Feel Anything When I Do This?)

ROBERT SHECKLEY

PAN BOOKS LTD
LONDON AND SYDNEY

First published in Great Britain 1972 as *Can You
Feel Anything When I Do This?* by Victor Gollancz Ltd
This edition published 1974 by Pan Books Ltd,
Cavaye Place, London SW10 9PG

ISBN 0 330 23988 0

© Robert Sheckley 1961, 1968, 1969, 1970, 1971

Ten of the stories included in this collection were originally
published in magazines as follows:

'Can You Feel Anything When I Do This?', 'Cordle to
Onion to Carrot', 'The Same to You Doubled', and 'Pas
de Trois of the Chef and the Waiter and the Customer' (this
last story under the title of 'Three Sinners in the Green Jade
Moon') in *Playboy*; 'The Petrified World' in *IF*; 'The Cruel
Equations' and 'Tripout' in *BOAC*; 'Starting from Scratch'
and 'Tailpipe to Disaster' in *The Magazine of Fantasy and
Science Fiction*; and 'Down the Digestive Tract and into the
Cosmos with Mantra, Tantra, and Specklebang' (under
the title of 'Down the Digestive Tract') in *Galaxy*.

*Made and printed in Great Britain by
Cox & Wyman Ltd, London, Reading and Fakenham*

TABLE OF CONTENTS

To Abby

The Same to You Doubled

In New York, it never fails, the doorbell rings just when
you've plopped down on to the couch for a well-deserved
snooze. Now, a person of character would say, 'To hell with
that, a man's home is his castle and they can slide any tele-
grams under the door.' But if you're like Edelstein, not
particularly strong on character, then you think to yourself
that maybe it's the blonde from 12C who has come up to
borrow a jar of chili powder. Or it could even be some crazy
film producer who wants to make a movie based on the
letters you've been sending your mother in Santa Monica.
(And why not; don't they make movies out of worse material than that?)

Yet this time, Edelstein had really decided not to answer
the bell. Lying on the couch, his eyes still closed, he called
out, 'I don't want any.'

'Yes you do,' a voice from the other side of the door
replied.

'I've got all the encyclopaedias, brushes and waterless
cookery I need,' Edelstein called back wearily. 'Whatever
you've got, I've got it already.'

'Look,' the voice said, 'I'm not selling anything. I want to
give you something.'

Edelstein smiled the thin, sour smile of the New Yorker
who knows that if someone made him a gift of a package of
genuine, unmarked $20 bills, he'd still somehow end up
having to pay for it.

'If it's *free*,' Edelstein answered, 'then I *definitely* can't afford it.'

'But I mean *really* free,' the voice said. 'I mean free that it won't cost you anything now or ever.'

'I'm not interested,' Edelstein replied, admiring his firmness of character.

The voice did not answer.

Edelstein called out, 'Hey, if you're still there, please go away.'

'My dear Mr Edelstein,' the voice said, 'cynicism is merely a form of naïveté. Mr Edelstein, wisdom is discrimination.'

'He gives me lectures now,' Edelstein said to the wall.

'All right,' the voice said, 'forget the whole thing, keep your cynicism and your racial prejudice; do I need this kind of trouble?'

'Just a minute,' Edelstein answered. 'What makes you think I'm prejudiced?'

'Let's not crap around,' the voice said. 'If I was raising funds for Hadassah or selling Israel bonds, it would have been different. But, obviously, I am what I am, so excuse me for living.'

'Not so fast,' Edelstein said. 'As far as I'm concerned, you're just a voice from the other side of the door. For all I know, you could be Catholic or Seventh-Day Adventist or even Jewish.'

'*You knew*,' the voice responded.

'Mister, I swear to you—'

'Look,' the voice said, 'it doesn't matter, I come up against a lot of this kind of thing. Goodbye, Mr Edelstein.'

'Just a minute,' Edelstein replied.

He cursed himself for a fool. How often had he fallen for some huckster's line, ending up, for example, paying $9.98 for an illustrated two-volume *Sexual History of Mankind*, which his friend Manowitz had pointed out he could have brought in any Marboro bookstore for $2.98?

But the voice was right. Edelstein had somehow known that he was dealing with a goy.

And the voice would go away thinking, *The Jews, they think they're better than everyone else*. Further, he would tell this to his bigoted friends at the next meeting of the Elks or the Knights of Columbus, and there it would be, another black eye for the Jews.

'I do have a weak character,' Edelstein thought sadly.

He called out, 'All right! You can come in! But I warn you from the start, I am not going to buy anything.'

He pulled himself to his feet and started walking towards the door. Then he stopped, for the voice had replied, 'Thank you very much,' and then a man had walked through the closed, double-locked wooden door.

The man was of medium height, nicely dressed in a grey pin-stripe modified Edwardian suit. His cordovan boots were highly polished. He was black, carried a briefcase, and he had stepped through Edelstein's door as if it had been made of Jell-O.

'Just a minute, stop, hold on one minute,' Edelstein said. He found that he was clasping both of his hands together and his heart was beating unpleasantly fast.

The man stood perfectly still and at his ease, one yard within the apartment. Edelstein started to breathe again. He said, 'Sorry, I just had a brief attack, a kind of hallucination—'

'Want to see me do it again?' the man asked.

'My God, no! So you *did* walk through the door! Oh, God, I think I'm in trouble.'

Edelstein went back to the couch and sat down heavily. The man sat down in a nearby chair.

'What is this all about?' Edelstein whispered.

'I do the door thing to save time,' the man said. 'It usually closes the credulity gap. My name is Charles Sitwell. I am a field man for the Devil.'

Edelstein believed him. He tried to think of a prayer, but all he could remember was the one he used to say over bread in the summer camp he had attended when he was a boy. It probably wouldn't help. He also knew the Lord's Prayer, but that wasn't even his religion. Perhaps the salute to the flag . . .

'Don't get all worked up,' Sitwell said. 'I'm not here after your soul or any old-fashioned crap like that.'

'How can I believe you?' Edelstein asked.

'Figure it out for yourself,' Sitwell told him. 'Consider only the war aspect. Nothing but rebellions and revolutions for the past fifty years or so. For us, that means an unprecedented supply of condemned Americans, Viet Cong, Nigerians, Biafrans, Indonesians, South Africans, Russians, Indians, Pakistanis and Arabs. Israelis, too, I'm sorry to tell you. Also, we're pulling in more Chinese than usual, and just recently, we've begun to get plenty of action on the South American market. Speaking frankly, Mr Edelstein, we're overloaded with souls. If another war starts this year, we'll have to declare an amnesty on venial sins.'

Edelstein thought it over. 'Then you're really not here to take me to hell?'

'Hell, no!' Sitwell said. 'I told you, our waiting list is longer than for Peter Cooper Village; we hardly have any room left in limbo.'

'Well . . . Then why are you here?'

Sitwell crossed his legs and leaned forward earnestly. 'Mr Edelstein, you have to understand that hell is very much like US Steel or IT & T. We're a big outfit and we're more or less a monopoly. But, like any really big corporation, we are imbued with the ideal of public service and we like to be well thought of.'

'Makes sense,' Edelstein said.

'But, unlike Ford, we can't very well establish a foundation and start giving out scholarships and work grants. People wouldn't understand. For the same reason, we can't start building model cities or fighting pollution. We can't even throw up a dam in Afghanistan without someone questioning our motives.'

'I see where it could be a problem,' Edelstein admitted.

'Yet we like to do something. So, from time to time, but especially now, with business so good, we like to distribute a small bonus to a random selection of potential customers.'

'Customer? Me?'

'No one is calling you a sinner,' Sitwell pointed out. 'I said *potential* – which means everybody.'

'Oh . . . What kind of bonus?'

'Three wishes,' Sitwell said briskly. 'That's the traditional form.'

'Let me see if I've got this straight,' Edelstein said. 'I can have any three wishes I want? With no penalty, no secret ifs and buts?'

'There is one but,' Sitwell said.

'I knew it,' Edelstein said.

'It's simple enough. Whatever you wish for, your worst enemy gets double.'

Edelstein thought about that. 'So if I asked for a million dollars—'

'Your worst enemy would get two million dollars.'

'And if I asked for pneumonia?'

'Your worst enemy would get double pneumonia.'

Edelstein pursed his lips and shook his head. 'Look, not that I mean to tell you people how to run your business, but I hope you realize that you endanger customer good will with a clause like that.'

'It's a risk, Mr Edelstein, but absolutely necessary on a couple of counts,' Sitwell said. 'You see, the clause is a psychic feedback device that acts to maintain homeostasis.'

'Sorry, I'm not following you,' Edelstein answered.

'Let me put it this way. The clause acts to reduce the power of the three wishes and, thus, to keep things reasonably normal. A wish is an extremely strong instrument, you know.'

'I can imagine,' Edelstein said. 'Is there a second reason?'

'You should have guessed it already,' Sitwell said, baring exceptionally white teeth in an approximation of a smile. 'Clauses like that are our trade mark. That's how you know it's a genuine hellish product.'

'I see, I see,' Edelstein said. 'Well, I'm going to need some time to think about this.'

'The offer is good for thirty days,' Sitwell said, standing up. 'When you want to make a wish, simply state it – clearly and loudly. I'll attend to the rest.'

Sitwell walked to the door. Edelstein said, 'There's only one problem I think I should mention.'

'What's that?' Sitwell asked.

'Well, it just so happens that I don't have a worst enemy. In fact, I don't have an enemy in the world.'

Sitwell laughed hard, then wiped his eyes with a mauve handkerchief. 'Edelstein,' he said, 'you're really too much! Not an enemy in the world! What about your cousin Seymour, who you wouldn't lend five hundred dollars to, to start a dry-cleaning business? Is he a friend all of a sudden?'

'I hadn't thought about Seymour,' Edelstein answered.

'And what about Mrs Abramowitz, who spits at the mention of your name, because you wouldn't marry her Marjorie? What about Tom Cassidy in apartment 1C of this building, who has a complete collection of Goebbels' speeches and dreams every night of killing all of the Jews in the world, beginning with you? ... Hey, are you all right?'

Edelstein, sitting on the couch, had gone white and his hands were clasped tightly together again.

'I never realized,' he said.

'No one realizes,' Sitwell said. 'Look, take it easy, six or seven enemies is nothing; I can assure you that you're well below average, hatewise.'

'Who else?' Edelstein asked, breathing heavily.

'I'm not going to tell you,' Sitwell said. 'It would be needless aggravation.'

'But I have to know who is my worst enemy! Is it Cassiday? So you think I should buy a gun?'

Sitwell shook his head. 'Cassiday is a harmless, half-witted lunatic. He'll never lift a finger, you have my word on that. Your worst enemy is a man named Edward Samuel Manowitz.'

'You're sure of that?' Elstein asked incredulously.

'Completely sure.'

'But Manowitz happens to be my best friend.'

'Also your worst enemy,' Sitwell replied. 'Sometimes it works like that. Goodbye, Mr Edelstein, and good luck with your three wishes.'

'Wait!' Edelstein cried. He wanted to ask a million questions; but he was embarrassed and he asked only, 'How can it be that hell is so crowded?'

'Because only heaven is infinite,' Sitwell told him.

'You know about heaven, too?'

'Of course. It's the parent corporation. But now I really must be getting along. I have an appointment in Poughkeepsie. Good luck, Mr Edelstein.'

Sitwell waved and turned and walked out through the locked solid door.

Edelstein sat perfectly still for five minutes. He thought about Eddie Manowitz. His worst enemy! That was laughable; hell had really gotten its wires crossed on that piece of information. He had known Manowitz for twenty years, saw him nearly every day, played chess and gin rummy with him. They went for walks together, saw movies together, at least one night a week they ate dinner together.

It was true, of course, that Manowitz could sometimes open up a big mouth and overstep the boundaries of good taste.

Sometimes Manowitz could be downright rude.

To be perfectly honest, Manowitz had, on more than one occasion, been insulting.

'But we're *friends*,' Edelstein said to himself. 'We *are* friends, aren't we?'

There was an easy way to test it, he realized. He could wish for $1,000,000. That would give Manowitz $2,000,000. But so what? Would he, a wealthy man, care that his best friend was wealthier?

Yes! He would care! He damned well would care! It would eat his life away if a wise guy like Manowitz got rich on Edelstein's wish.

'My God!' Edelstein thought. 'An hour ago, I was a poor but contented man. Now I have three wishes and an enemy.'

He found that he was twisting his hands together again. He shook his head. This was going to need some thought.

In the next week, Edelstein managed to get a leave of absence from his job and sat day and night with a pen and pad in his hand. At first, he couldn't get his mind off castles. Castles seemed to *go* with wishes. But, on second thought, it was not a simple matter. Taking an average dream castle with a ten-foot-thick stone wall, grounds and the rest, one had to consider the matter of upkeep. There was heating to worry about, the cost of several servants, because anything less would look ridiculous.

So it came at last to a matter of money.

I could keep up a pretty decent castle on $2000 a week, Edelstein thought, jotting figures down rapidly on his pad.

But that would mean that Manowitz would be maintaining two castles on $4000 a week!

By the second week, Edelstein had gotten past castles and was speculating feverishly on the endless possibilities and combinations of travel. Would it be too much to ask for a cruise around the world? Perhaps it would; he wasn't even sure he was up to it. Surely he could accept a summer in Europe? Even a two-week vacation at the Fontainebleau in Miami Beach to rest his nerves.

But Manowitz would get two vacations! If Edelstein stayed at the Fontainebleau, Manowitz would have a penthouse suite at the Key Largo Colony Club. Twice.

It was almost better to stay poor and to keep Manowitz deprived.

Almost, but not quite.

During the final week, Edelstein was getting angry and desperate, even cynical. He said to himself, I'm an idiot, how do I know that there's anything to this? So Sitwell could walk through doors; does that make him a magician? Maybe I've been worried about nothing.

He surprised himself by standing up abruptly and saying,

in a loud, firm voice, 'I want twenty thousand dollars and I want it right now.'

He felt a gentle tug at his right buttock. He pulled out his wallet. Inside it, he found a certified check made out to him for $20,000.

He went down to his bank and cashed the check, trembling, certain that the police would grab him. The manager looked at the check and initialed it. The teller asked him what denominations he wanted it in. Edelstein told the teller to credit it to his account.

As he left the bank, Manowitz came rushing in, an expression of fear, joy and bewilderment on his face.

Edelstein hurried home before Manowitz could speak to him. He had a pain in his stomach for the rest of the day.

Idiot! He had asked for only a lousy $20,000. But Manowitz had gotten $40,000!

A man could die from the aggravation.

Edelstein spent his days alternating between apathy and rage. That pain in the stomach had come back, which meant that he was probably giving himself an ulcer.

It was all so damned unfair! Did he have to push himself into an early grave, worrying about Manowitz?

Yes!

For now he realized that Manowitz was really his enemy and that the thought of enriching his enemy was literally killing him.

He thought about that and then said to himself, Edelstein, listen to me; you can't go on like this, you must get some satisfaction!

But how?

He paced up and down his apartment. The pain was definitely an ulcer; what else could it be?

Then it came to him. Edelstein stopped pacing. His eyes rolled wildly and, seizing paper and pencil, he made some lightning calculations. When he finished, he was flushed, excited – happy for the first time since Sitwell's visit.

He stood up. He shouted, 'I want six hundred pounds of chopped chicken liver and I want it at once!'

The caterers began to arrive within five minutes.

Edelstein ate several giant portions of chopped chicken liver, stored two pounds of it in his refrigerator and sold most of the rest to a caterer at half price, making over $700 on the deal. The janitor had to take away 75 pounds that had been overlooked. Edelstein had a good laugh at the thought of Manowitz standing in his apartment up to his neck in chopped chicken liver.

His enjoyment was short-lived. He learned that Manowitz had kept ten pounds for himself (the man always had had a gross appetite), presented five pounds to a drab little widow he was trying to make an impression on and sold the rest back to the caterer for one third off, earning over $2000.

I am the world's prize imbecile, Edelstein thought. For a minute's stupid satisfaction, I gave up a wish worth conservatively $100,000,000. And what do I get out of it? Two pounds of chopped chicken liver, a few hundred dollars and the lifelong friendship of my janitor!

He knew he was killing himself from sheer brute aggravation.

He was down to one wish now.

And now it was *crucial* that he spend that final wish wisely. But he had to ask for something that he wanted desperately – something that Manowitz would *not* like at all.

Four weeks had gone by. One day, Edelstein realized glumly that his time was just about up. He had racked his brain, only to confirm his worst suspicions: Manowitz liked everything that he liked. Manowitz liked castles, women, wealth, cars, vacations, wine, music, food. Whatever you named, Manowitz the copycat liked it.

Then he remembered: Manowitz, by some strange quirk of taste buds, could not abide lox.

But Edelstein didn't like lox, either, not even Nova Scotia.

Edelstein prayed: Dear God, who is in charge of hell and heaven, I have had three wishes and used two miserably. Listen, God, I don't mean to be ungrateful, but I ask you, if a man happens to be granted three wishes, shouldn't he be able to do better for himself than I have done? Shouldn't he be able to have something good happen to him without filling the pockets of Manowitz, his worst enemy, who does nothing but collect double with no effort or pain?

The final hour arrived. Edelstein grew calm, in the manner of a man who had accepted his fate. He realized that his hatred of Manowitz was futile, unworthy of him. With a new and sweet serenity, he said to himself. I am now going to ask for what I, Edelstein, personally want. If Manowitz has to go along for the ride, it simply can't be helped.

Edelstein stood up very straight. He said, 'This is my last wish. I've been a bachelor too long. What I want is a woman whom I can marry. She should be about five feet, four inches tall, weigh about 115 pounds, shapely, of course, and with naturally blonde hair. She should be intelligent, practical, in love with me, Jewish, of course, but sensual and fun-loving—'

The Edelstein mind suddenly moved into high gear!

'And *especially*,' he added, 'she should be – I don't know quite how to put this – she should be the *most*, the *maximum*, that I want and can handle, speaking now in a purely sexual sense. You understand what I mean, Sitwell? Delicacy forbids that I should spell it out more specifically than that, but if the matter must be explained to you . . .'

There was a light, somehow *sexual* tapping at the door. Edelstein went to answer it, chuckling to himself. Over twenty thousand dollars, two pounds of chopped chicken liver and now this! Manowitz, he thought, I have you now: Double the most a man wants is something I probably shouldn't have wished on my worst enemy, but I did.

Cordle to Onion to Carrot

Surely, you remember that bully who kicked sand on the seven-stone weakling? Well, that puny man's problem has never been solved, despite Charles Atlas's claims to the contrary. A genuine bully *likes* to kick sand on people; for him, simply, there is gut-deep satisfaction in a put-down. It wouldn't matter if you weighed seventeen stone – all of it rock-hard muscle and steely sinew – and were as wise as Solomon or as witty as Voltaire; you'd still end up with the sand of an insult in your eyes, and probably you wouldn't do anything about it.

That was how Howard Cordle viewed the situation. He was a pleasant man who was for ever being pushed around by Fuller Brush men, fund solicitors, head waiters and other imposing figures of authority. Cordle hated it. He suffered in silence the countless numbers of manic-aggressives who shoved their way to the heads of lines, took taxis he had hailed first and sneeringly steered away girls to whom he was talking at parties.

What made it worse was that these people seemed to welcome provocation, to go looking for it, all for the sake of causing discomfort to others.

Cordle couldn't understand why this should be, until one midsummer's day, when he was driving through the northern regions of Spain while stoned out of his mind, the god Thoth-Hermes granted him original enlightenment by murmuring, 'Uh, look, I groove with the problem, baby, but dig, we gotta put carrots in or it ain't no stew.'

'*Carrots*?' said Cordle, struggling for illumination.

'I'm talking about those types who get you uptight,' Thoth-Hermes explained. 'They *gotta* act that way, baby, on account of they're carrots, and that's how carrots are.'

'If they are carrots,' Cordle said, feeling his way, 'then I—'

'You, of course, are a little pearly-white onion.'

'Yes! My God, yes!' Cordle cried, dazzled by the blinding light of *satori*.

'And, naturally, you and all the other pearly-white onions think that carrots are just bad news, merely some kind of mis-shapen, orangey onion; whereas the carrots look at you and rap about *freaky round white carrots, wow*! I mean, you're just too much for each other, whereas, in actuality—'

'Yes, go on!' cried Cordle.

'In actuality,' Thoth-Hermes declared, '*everything's got a place in The Stew*!'

'Of course! I see, I see, I see!'

'And *that* means that everybody who exists is necessary, and you *must* have long hateful orange carrots if you're also going to have nice pleasant decent white onions, or vice versa, because without all of the ingredients, it isn't a Stew, which is to say, life, it becomes, uh, let me see . . .'

'A soup!' cried ecstatic Cordle.

'You're coming in five by five,' chanted Thoth-Hermes. 'Lay down the word, deacon, and let the people know the divine formula . . .'

'A *soup*!' said Cordle. 'Yes, I see it now – creamy, pure-white onion soup is our dream of heaven, whereas fiery orange carrot broth is our notion of hell. It fits, it all fits together!'

'Om manipadme hum,' intoned Thoth-Hermes.

'But where do the green peas go? What about the *meat* for God's sake?'

'Don't pick at the metaphor,' Thoth-Hermes advised him 'it leaves a nasty scab. Stick with the carrots and onions And, here, let me offer you a drink – a house specialty.'

'But the spices, where do you put the *spices*?' Cordle demanded, taking a long swig of burgundy-coloured liquid from a rusted canteen.

'Baby, you're asking questions that can be revealed only to a thirteenth-degree Mason with piles, wearing sandals. Sorry about that. Just remember that everything goes into The Stew.'

'Into The Stew,' Cordle repeated, smacking his lips.

'And, especially, stick with the carrots and onions, you were really grooving there.'

'Carrots and onions,' Cordle repeated.

'That's your trip.' Thoth-Hermes said. 'Hey, we've gotten to Corunna; you can let me out anywhere around here.'

Cordle pulled his rented car off the road. Thoth-Hermes took his knapsack from the back seat and got out.

'Thanks for the lift, baby.'

'My pleasure. Thank *you* for the wine. What kind did you say it was?'

'*Vino de casa* mixed with a mere smidgen of old Dr Hammerfinger's essence of instant powdered Power-Pack brand acid. Brewed by gnurrs in the secret laboratories of UCLA in preparation for the big all-Europe turn-on.'

'Whatever it was, it surely *was*,' Cordle said deeply. 'Pure elixir to me. You could sell neckties to antelopes with that stuff; you could change the world from an oblate spheroid into a truncated trapezoid . . . What did I say?'

'Never mind, it's all part of your trip. Maybe you better lie down for a while, huh?'

'Where gods command, mere mortals must obey,' Cordle said iambically. He lay down on the front seat of the car. Thoth-Hermes bent over him, his beard burnished gold, his head wreathed in plane trees.

'You OK?'

'Never better in my life.'

'Want me to stand by?'

'Unnecessary. You have helped me beyond potentiality.'

'Glad to hear it, baby, you're making a fine sound. You really are OK? Well, then, ta.'

Thoth-Hermes marched off into the sunset. Cordle closed his eyes and solved various problems that had perplexed the greatest philosophers of all ages. He was mildly surprised at how simple complexity was.

At last he went to sleep. He awoke some six hours later. He had forgotten most of his brilliant insights, the lucid solutions. It was inconceivable: How can one misplace the keys of the universe? But he had, and there seemed no hope of reclaiming them. Paradise was lost for good.

He did remember about the onions and the carrots, though, and he remembered The Stew. It was not the sort of insight he might have chosen if he'd had any choice; but this was what had come to him, and he did not reject it. Cordle knew, perhaps instinctively, that in the insight game, you take whatever you can get.

The next day, he reached Santander in a driving rain. He decided to write amusing letters to all of his friends, perhaps even try his hand at a travel sketch. That required a typewriter. The *conserje* at his hotel directed him to a store that rented out typewriters. He went there and found a clerk who spoke perfect English.

'Do you rent typewriters by the day?' Cordle asked.

'Why not?' the clerk replied. He had oily black hair and a thin aristocratic nose.

'How much for that one?' Cordle, indicating a thirty-year-old Erika portable.

'Seventy pesetas a day, which is to say, one dollar. Usually.'

'Isn't this usually?'

'Certainly not, since you are a foreigner in transit. For you, one hundred and eighty pesetas a day.'

'All right,' Cordle said, reaching for his wallet. 'I'd like to have it for two days.'

'I shall also require your passport and a deposit of fifty dollars.'

Cordle attempted a mild joke. 'Hey, I just want to type on it, not marry it.'

The clerk shrugged.

'Look, the *conserje* has my passport at the hotel. How about taking my driver's licence instead?'

'Certainly not. I must hold your passport, in case you decide to default.'

'But why do you need my passport *and* the deposit?' Cordle asked, feeling bullied and ill at ease. 'I mean, look, the machine's not worth twenty dollars.'

'You are an expert, perhaps, in the Spanish market value of used German typewriters?'

'No but—'

'Then permit me, sir, to conduct my business as I see fit. I will also need to know the use to which you plan to put the machine.'

'The *use*?'

'Of course, the use.'

It was one of these preposterous foreign situations that can happen to anyone. The clerk's request was incomprehensible and his manner was insulting. Cordle was about to give a curt little nod, turn on his heel and walk out.

Then he remembered about the onions and carrots. He saw The Stew. And suddenly, it occurred to Cordle that he could be whatever vegetable he wanted to be.

He turned to the clerk. He smiled winningly. He said, 'You wish to know the use I will make of the typewriter?'

'Exactly.'

'Well,' Cordle said, 'quite frankly, I had planned to stuff it up my nose.'

The clerk gaped at him.

'It's quite a successful method of smuggling,' Cordle went on. 'I was also planning to give you a stolen passport and counterfeit pesetas. Once I got into Italy, I would have sold the typewriter for ten thousand dollars. Milan is undergoing a typewriter famine, you know; they're desperate, they'll buy anything.'

'Sir,' the clerk said, 'you choose to be disagreeable.'

'Nasty is the word you were looking for. I've changed my mind about the typewriter. But let me compliment you on your command of English.'

'I have studied assiduously,' the clerk admitted, with a hint of pride.

'That is evident. And, despite a certain weakness in the Rs, you succeed in sounding like a Venetian gondolier with a cleft palate. My best wishes to your esteemed family. I leave you now to pick your pimples in peace.'

Reviewing the scene later, Cordle decided that he had performed quite well in his maiden appearance as a carrot. True, his closing lines had been a little forced and over-intellectualized. But the undertone of viciousness had been convincing.

Most important was the simple resounding fact that he had done it. And now, in the quiet of his hotel room, instead of churning his guts in a frenzy of self-loathing, he had the tranquilizing knowledge of having put someone else in that position.

He had done it! Just like that, he had transformed himself from onion into carrot!

But was his position ethically defensible? Presumably, the clerk could not help being detestable; he was a product of his own genetic and social environment, a victim of his conditioning; he was naturally rather than intentionally hateful—

Cordle stopped himself. He saw that he was engaged in typical onionish thinking, which was an inability to conceive of carrots except as an aberration from oniondom.

But now he knew that both onions *and* carrots had to exist; otherwise, there would be no Stew.

And he also knew that a man was free and could choose whatever vegetable he wanted to be. He could even live as an amusing little green pea, or a gruff, forceful clove of garlic (though perhaps that was scratching at the metaphor). In any event, a man could take his pick between carrothood and oniondom.

There is much to think about here, Cordle thought. But he never got around to thinking about it. Instead, he went sight-seeing, despite the rain, and then continued his travels.

The next incident occurred in Nice, in a cosy little restaurant on the Avenue des Diables Bleus, with red-chequered table-cloths and incomprehensible menus written in longhand with purple ink. There were four waiters, one of whom looked like Jean-Paul Belmondo, down to the cigarette drooping from his lower lip. The others looked like run-of-the-mill muggers. There were several Scandinavian customers quietly eating a *cassoulet*, one old Frenchman in a beret and three homely English girls.

Belmondo sauntered over. Cordle, who spoke a clear though idiomatic French, asked for the ten-franc menu he had seen hanging in the window.

The waiter gave him the sort of look one reserves for pretentious beggars. 'Ah, that is all finished for today,' he said, and handed Cordle a thirty-franc menu.

In his previous incarnation, Cordle would have bit down on the bullet and ordered. Or possibly he would have risen, trembling with outrage, and left the restaurant, blundering into a chair on the way.

But now—

'Perhaps you did not understand me,' Cordle said. 'It is a matter of French law that you must serve from all of the fixed-price menus that you show in the window.'

'*M'sieu* is a lawyer?' the waiter inquired, his hands perched insolently on his hips.

'No. *M'sieu* is a troublemaker,' Cordle said, giving what he considered to be fair warning.

'Then *m'sieu* must make what trouble he desires,' the waiter said. His eyes were slits.

'OK,' Cordle said. And just then, fortuitously, an elderly couple came into the restaurant. The man wore a double-breasted slate-blue suit with a half-inch white pin stripe. The woman wore a flowered organdy dress. Cordle called to them, 'Excuse me, are you folks English?'

A bit startled, the man inclined his head in the barest intimation of a nod.

'Then I would advise you not to eat here. I am a health inspector for UNESCO. The chef apparently has not washed his hands since D-day. We haven't made a definitive test for typhoid yet, but we have our suspicions. As soon as my assistant arrives with the litmus paper . . .'

A deathly hush had fallen over the restaurant.

'I suppose a boiled egg would be safe enough,' Cordle said.

The elderly man probably didn't believe him. But it didn't matter, Cordle was obviously trouble.

'Come, Mildred,' he said, and they hurried out.

'There goes sixty francs plus five per cent tip,' Cordle said, coolly.

'Leave here at once!' the waiter snarled.

'I like it here,' Cordle said, folding his arms. 'I like the *ambiance*, the sense of intimacy—'

'You are not permitted to stay without eating.'

'I shall eat. From the ten-franc menu.'

The waiters looked at one another, nodded in unison and began to advance in a threatening phalanx. Cordle called to the other diners, 'I ask you all to bear witness! These men are going to attack me, four against one, contrary to French law and universal human ethics, simply because I want to order from the ten-franc menu, which they have falsely advertised.'

It was a long speech, but this was clearly the time for grandiloquence. Cordle repeated it in English.

The English girls gasped. The old Frenchman went on eating his soup. The Scandinavians nodded grimly and began to take off their jackets.

The waiters held another conference. The one who looked like Belmondo said, '*M'sieu*, you are forcing us to call the police.'

'That will save me the trouble,' Cordle said, 'of calling them myself.'

'Surely, *m'sieu* does not want to spend his holiday in court?'

'That is how *m'sieu* spends most of his holidays,' Cordle said.

The waiters conferred again. Then Belmondo stalked over with the thirty-franc menu. 'The cost of the *prix fixe* will be ten francs, since evidently that is all *m'sieu* can afford.'

Cordle let that pass. 'Bring me onion soup, green salad and the *boeuf bourguignon*.'

The waiter went to put in the order. While he was waiting, Cordle sang *Waltzing Matilda* in a moderately loud voice. He suspected it might speed up the service. He got his food by the time he reached 'You'll never catch me alive, said he' for the second time. Cordle pulled the tureen of stew towards him and lifted a spoon.

It was a breathless moment. Not one diner had left the restaurant. And Cordle was prepared. He leaned forward, soup spoon in shovelling position, and sniffed delicately. A hush fell over the room.

'It lacks a certain something,' Cordle said aloud. Frowning, he poured the onion soup into the *boeuf bourguignon*. He sniffed, shook his head and added a half loaf of bread, in slices. He sniffed again and added the salad and the contents of a salt cellar.

Cordle pursued his lips. 'No,' he said, 'it simply will not do.'

He overturned the entire contents of the tureen on to the table. It was an act comparable, perhaps, to throwing gentian violet on the *Mona Lisa*. All of France and most of western Switzerland went into a state of shock.

Unhurriedly, but keeping the frozen waiters under surveillance, Cordle rose and dropped ten francs into the mess. He walked to the door, turned and said, 'My compliments to the chef, who might better be employed as a cement mixer. And this, *mon vieux*, is for you.'

He threw his crumpled linen napkin on to the floor.

As the matador, after a fine series of passes, turns his back contemptuously on the bull and strolls away, so went Cordle. For some unknown reason, the waiters did not rush

out after him, shoot him dead and hang his corpse from the
nearest lamp post. So Cordle walked for ten or fifteen
blocks, taking rights and lefts at random. He came to the
Promenade des Anglais and sat down on a bench. He was
trembling and his shirt was drenched with perspiration.

'But I did it,' he said. 'I did it! I! I was unspeakably vile
and I got away with it!'

Now he really knew why carrots acted that way. Dear
God in heaven, what joy, what delectable bliss!

Cordle then reverted to his mild-mannered self, smoothly
and without regrets. He stayed that way until his second day
in Rome.

He was in his rented car. He and seven other drivers were
lined up at a traffic light on the Corso Vittorio Emanuele II
There were perhaps twenty cars behind them. All of the
drivers were revving their engines, hunched over their steer
ing wheels with slitted eyes, dreaming of Le Mans. All
except Cordle, who was drinking in the cyclopean archi
tecture of downtown Rome. The chequered flag came down
The drivers floored their accelerators, trying to spin the
wheels of their underpowered Fiats, wearing out their
clutches and their nerves, but doing so with *éclat* and *brio*
All except Cordle, who seemed to be the only man in Rome
who didn't have to win a race or keep an appointment.

Without undue haste or particular delay, Cordle de
pressed the clutch and engaged the gear. Already he had
lost nearly two seconds – unthinkable at Monza or Monte
Carlo.

The driver behind him blew his horn frantically.

Cordle smiled to himself, a secret, ugly expression. He pu
the gears into neutral, engaged the hand brake and stepped
out of his car. He ambled over to the horn-blower, who had
turned pasty white and was fumbling under his seat, hoping
to find a crow-bar.

'Yes?' said Cordle, in French, 'is something wrong?'

'No, no, nothing,' the driver replied in French – his firs
mistake. 'I merely wanted you to go, to move.'

'But I was just doing that,' Cordle pointed out.

'Well, then! It is all right!'

'No, it is not all right,' Cordle told him. 'I think I deserve a better explanation of why you blew your horn at me.'

The horn-blower – a Milanese businessman on holiday with his wife and four children – rashly replied, 'My dear sir, you were slow, you were delaying us all.'

'*Slow*?' said Cordle. 'You blew your horn two seconds after the light changed. Do you call two seconds slow?'

'It was much longer than that,' the man riposted feebly.

Traffic was now backed up as far south as Naples. A crowd of ten thousand had gathered. *Carabinieri* units in Viterbo and Genoa had been called into a state of alert.

'That is untrue,' Cordle said. 'I have witnesses.' He gestured at the crowd, which gestured back. 'I shall call my witnesses before the courts. You must know that you broke the law by blowing your horn within the city limits of Rome in what was clearly not an emergency.'

The Milanese businessman looked at the crowd, now swollen to perhaps fifty thousand. Dear God, he thought, if only the Goths would descend again and exterminate these leering Romans! If only the ground would open up and swallow this insane Frenchman! If only he, Giancarlo Morelli, had a dull spoon with which to open up the veins of his wrist!

Jets from the Sixth Fleet thundered overhead, hoping to avert the long-expected *coup d'état*.

The Milanese businessman's own wife was shouting abuse at him: Tonight he would cut out her faithless heart and mail it back to her mother

What was there to do? In Milan, he would have had this Frenchman's head on a platter. But this was Rome, a southern city, an unpredictable and dangerous place. And legalistically, he was possibly in the wrong, which left him at a further disadvantage in the argument.

'Very well,' he said. 'The blowing of the horn was perhaps truly unnecessary, despite the provocation.'

'I insist on a genuine apology,' insisted Cordle.

There was a thundering sound to the east: Thousands of
Soviet tanks were moving into battle formation across the
plains of Hungary, ready to resist the long-expected NATO
thrust into Transylvania. The water supply was cut off in
Foggia, Brindisi, Bari. The Swiss closed their frontiers and
stood ready to dynamite the passes.

'All right, I apologize!' the Milanese businessman
screamed. 'I am sorry I provoked you and even sorrier that I
was born! Again, I apologize! Now will you go away and let
me have a heart attack in peace?'

'I accept your apology,' Cordle said. 'No hard feelings,
eh?' He strolled back to his car, humming *Blow the Man
Down*, and drove away as millions cheered.

War was once again averted by a hairbreadth.

Cordle drove to the Arch of Titus, parked his car and – to
the sound of a thousand trumpets – passed through it. He
deserved this triumph as well as any Caesar.

God, he gloated, I was *loathsome!*

In England, Cordle stepped on a young lady's toe just inside
the Traitors' Gate of the Tower of London. This should
have served as an intimation of something. The young lady
was named Mavis. She came from Short Hills, New Jersey
and she had long straight dark hair. She was slender, pretty
intelligent, energetic and she had a sense of humour. She had
minor faults, as well, but they play no part in this story. She
let Cordle buy her a cup of coffee. They were together con-
stantly for the rest of the week.

'I think I am infatuated,' Cordle said to himself on the
seventh day. He realized at once that he had made a slight
understatement. He was violently and hopelessly in love.

But what did Mavis feel? She seemed not unfond of him.
It was even possible that she might, conceivably, recipro-
cate.

At that moment, Cordle had a flash of prescience. He
realized that one week ago, he had stepped on the toe of his
future wife and mother of his two children, both of whom
would be born and brought up in a split-level house with

nflatable furniture in Summit, New Jersey, or possibly Mill-
urn.

This may sound unattractive and provincial when stated
aldly; but it was desirable to Cordle, who had no pre-
ensions to cosmopolitanism. After all, not all of us can live
t Cap Ferrat. Strangely enough, not all of us even want to.

That day, Cordle and Mavis went to the Marshall Gordon
Residence in Belgravia to see the Byzantine miniatures.
Mavis had a passion for Byzantine miniatures that seemed
armless enough at the time. The collection was private, but
Mavis had secured invitations through a local Avis man-
ger, who was trying very hard, indeed.

They came to the Gordon Residence, an awesome Re-
ency building in Huddlestone Mews. They rang. A butler
n full evening dress answered the door. They showed the
nvitations. The butler's glance and lifted eyebrow showed
hat they were carrying second-class invitations of the sort
iven to importunate art poseurs on seventeen-day all-
xpense economy flights, rather than the engraved first-class
nvitations given to Picasso, Jackie Onassis, Sugar Ray Rob-
nson, Norman Mailer, Charles Goren and other movers
nd shakers of the world.

The butler said, 'Oh, yes . . .' Two words that spoke black
olumes. His face twitched, he looked like a man who has
eceived an unexpected visit from Tamerlane and a regiment
f his Golden Horde.

'The miniatures,' Cordle reminded him.

'Yes, of course . . . But I am afraid, sir, that no one is
llowed into the Gordon Residence without a coat and
ecktie.'

It was an oppressive August day. Cordle was wearing a
ports shirt. He said, 'Did I hear you correctly? Coat and
ecktie?'

The butler said, 'That is the rule, sir.'

Mavis asked, 'Couldn't you make an exception this
nce?'

The butler shook his head. 'We really must stick by the
ules, miss. Otherwise . . .' He left the fear of vulgarity

T–B

unsaid, but it hung in the air like a chrome-plated fart.

'Of course,' Cordle said, pleasantly. 'Otherwise. So it's a coat and tie, is it? I think we can arrange that.'

Mavis put a hand on his arm and said, 'Howard, let's go. We can come back some other time.'

'Nonsense, my dear. If I may borrow your coat . . .'

He lifted the white raincoat from her shoulders and put it on, ripping a seam. 'There we go, mate!' he said briskly to the butler. 'That should do it, *n'est-ce pas*?'

'I think *not*,' the butler said, in a voice bleak enough to wither artichokes. 'In any event, there is the matter of the necktie.'

Cordle had been waiting for that. He whipped out his sweaty handkerchief and knotted it around his neck.

'Suiting you?' he leered, in an imitation of Peter Lorre as Mr Moto, which only he appreciated.

'*Howard! Let's go!*'

Cordle waited, smiling steadily at the butler, who was sweating for the first time in living memory.

'I'm afraid, sir, that that is not—'

'Not what?'

'Not precisely what was meant by coat and tie.'

'Are you trying to tell me,' Cordle said in a loud, unpleasant voice, 'that you are an arbiter of men's clothing as well as a door opener?'

'Of course not! But this impromptu attire—'

'What has "impromptu" got to do with it? Are people supposed to prepare three days in advance just to pass your inspection?'

'You are wearing a woman's water-proof and a soiled handkerchief,' the butler stated stiffly. 'I think there is no more to say.'

He began to close the door. Cordle said, 'You do that, sweetheart, and I'll have you up for slander and defamation of character. Those are serious charges over here, buddy, and I've got witnesses.'

Aside from Mavis, Cordle had collected a small, diffident but interested crowd.

'This is becoming entirely too ridiculous,' the butler said, temporizing, the door half closed.

'You'll find a stretch at Wormwood Scrubs even more ridiculous,' Cordle told him. 'I intend to persecute – I mean prosecute.'

'*Howard*!' cried Marvis.

He shook off her hand and fixed the butler with a piercing glance. He said, 'I am Mexican, though perhaps my excellent grasp of the English has deceived you. In my country, a man would cut his own throat before letting such an insult pass unavenged. A woman's coat, you say? *Hombre*, when I wear a coat, it becomes a *man's* coat. Or do you imply that I am a *maricón*, a – how do you say it? – homosexual?'

The crowd – becoming less modest – growled approval. Nobody except a lord loves a butler.

'I meant no such implication,' the butler said weakly.

'Then is it a man's coat?'

'Just as you wish, sir.'

'Unsatisfactory! The innuendo still exists. I go now to find an officer of the law.'

'Wait, let's not be hasty,' the butler said. His face was bloodless and his hands were shaking. 'Your coat is a man's coat, sir.'

'And what about my necktie?'

The butler made a final attempt at stopping Zapata and his blood-crazed peons.

'Well, sir, a handkerchief is demonstrably—'

'What I wear around my neck,' Cordle said coldly, 'becomes what it is intended to be. If I wore a piece of figured silk around my throat, would you call it ladies' underwear? Linen is a suitable material for a tie, *verdad*? Function defines terminology, don't you agree? If I ride to work on a cow, no one says that I am mounted on a steak. Or do you detect a flaw in my argument?'

'I'm afraid that I don't fully understand it . . .'

'Then how can you presume to stand in judgement over it?'

The crowd, which had been growing restless, now murmured approval.

'Sir,' cried the wretched butler, 'I beg of you . . .'

'*Otherwise*,' Cordle said with satisfaction, 'I have a coat, a necktie and an invitation. Perhaps you would be good enough to show us the Byzantine miniatures?'

The butler opened wide the door to Pancho Villa and his tattered hordes. The last bastion of civilization had been captured in less than an hour. Wolves howled along the banks of the Thames, Morelos' barefoot army stabled its horses in the British Museum, and Europe's long night had begun.

Cordle and Mavis viewed the collection in silence. They didn't exchange a word until they were alone and strolling through Regent's Park.

'Look, Mavis,' Cordle began.

'No, you look,' she said. 'You were horrible! You were unbelievable. You were – I can't find a word rotten enough for what you were! I never dreamed that you were one of those sadistic bastards who get their kicks out of humiliating people!'

'But, Mavis, you heard what he said to me, you heard the way—'

'He was a stupid, bigoted old man,' Mavis said. 'I thought you were not.'

'But he said—'

'It doesn't matter. The fact is, you were enjoying yourself!'

'Well, yes, maybe you're right,' Cordle said. 'Look, I can explain.'

'Not to me, you can't. Ever. Please stay away from me, Howard. Permanently. I mean that.'

The future mother of his two children began to walk away, out of his life. Cordle hurried after her.

'Mavis!'

'I'll call a cop, Howard, so help me, I will! Just leave me alone!'

'Mavis, I love you!'

She must have heard him, but she kept on walking. She
as a sweet and beautiful girl and definitely, unchangeably,
onion.

ordle was never able to explain to Mavis about The Stew
d about the necessity for experiencing behaviour before
ndemning it. Moments of mystical illumination are
dom explicable. He *was* able to make her believe that he
d undergone a brief psychotic episode, unique and unpre-
dented and – with her – never to be repeated.

They are married now, have one girl and one boy, live in a
it-level house in Plainfield, New Jersey, and are quite
ntent. Cordle is visibly pushed around by Fuller Brush
en, fund solicitors, head waiters and other imposing
ures of authority. But there is a difference.

Cordle makes a point of taking regularly scheduled, soli-
ry vacations. Last year, he made a small name for himself
Honolulu. This year, he is going to Buenos Aires.